KIMBALL THEATRE ORGAN

Cornelia Popa

Copyright © 2014 by Cornelia Popa
First Edition – 2014

ISBN
978-1-4602-4771-6 (Hardcover)
978-1-4602-4772-3 (Paperback)
978-1-4602-4773-0 (eBook)

Produced by:

FriesenPress

Suite 300 – 852 Fort Street
Victoria, BC, Canada V8W 1H8

www.friesenpress.com

Distributed to the trade by The Ingram Book Company

This work of fiction was inspired by the collection of the National Music Centre in Calgary, AB. Special thanks to their dedicated staff for sharing a love of music with children through their programming.

Visit http://www.nmc.ca to learn more

CHAPTER 1

I can't believe they really sent me away so they can have a vacation together! Jonathan Pearl couldn't keep his feet still. His whole body twitched from their nervous shuffle. He frowned and fixed his gaze at a spot on the carpet. *How could they do that to me and pretend they love me?* he had asked himself over and over again since the plane left San Diego. *Christmas is a family holiday; it's supposed to be spent with your parents, not your Grandma Joan and aunt's family! I haven't even been to their house before, what can I do there for two weeks? Sure, Grandma Joan is nice, but the rest of them I barely know – even a few Skype dates wouldn't make them more like family!*

"Please, return to your seats" the flight attendant's voice sounded on the speakers, "and put on your seatbelts. We are starting our descent into Edmonton."

Great! thought Jonathan. *Now I have to sit for another three hours or so in an old truck. Why do they have to live so far from the airport?*

"Hello, Johnny!" yelled Aunt Doris as soon as Jonathan entered the airport waiting area. "Welcome to Canada. I'm sure you'll like winter here!" she said hugging him. "Do you remember your cousin Anna? She's twelve now."

"Yes," Johnny said sharply, looking somewhere else.

"Well, let's go kids," said Aunt Doris stretching out her hand to touch Johnny's shoulder. "Are you tired, Johnny? Let me help you with the suitcase. You know, we and your Grandma Joan are so happy that you came to spend Christmas and New Years with us!"

Johnny pressed his lips into a tight line and looked down at his feet.

"I didn't want to come here!" Johnny's voice sounded strange even for himself. As he bent to catch his bag, fallen to the floor, he caught a glimpse of his cousin – Anna's big wide eyes and her stunned face melted his anger into sadness. "I didn't want to come here... alone." he said softly while tears filled his eyes.

"Johnny," said Aunt Doris. "You know we all love you. Your parents needed this time alone. It doesn't mean that they love you any less. Let's go home now, you'll feel better after a rest."

Through the car's window Johnny saw the snow covered trees running back and back ... *winter from the stories,* he thought, his eyelids feeling heavier and heavier.

"How old are you?" he heard a faraway voice. His eyelids were still heavy, but he turned slowly toward Anna and answered: "I'm eleven."

"We'll be home soon. Grandma Joan is making blueberry pie for dessert – and she only does that on special occasions." Anna paused and arranged her red coat with her hands. "It's my favorite, you know! Look, over there, it's our house."

Aunt Doris turned right off the main road into a paved alley with spruces on both sides. The house was big, with a sandstone façade and massive rock stairs. From the chimneys, white smoke went up in plumes. The sun appeared from behind the clouds and made the snow on top of the roof sparkle.

Aunt Doris opened the front door and let the kids inside the vast hall with a vaulted wooden ceiling from which hung an impressive crystal chandelier. The sun's rays shining through the upper windows deflected off its crystal prisms and made many little rainbows appear on the opposite wall. On the left, a door opened into a big room where Johnny could see a dining table already set up for lunch. On the right, there were three closed doors, while in front a grand staircase covered with a red carpet led to the upper floor.

"We're home, Mother!" Aunt Doris said, taking off her hat. Anna went to the first door on the right and opened it to hang up her coat: "Here's a hanger for you, Johnny."

The warmth in the house and the delicious smells coming from the kitchen softened Johnny. *She is nice, for a girl,* he thought. *Maybe we'll find something to play together while I have to stay here.*

From the dining room, Grandma Joan came to Johnny with her arms open. "Welcome, my dear. Oh, let me see you – you are so handsome! How was your trip? You know what? You'll tell me later, let me show you your room and then we'll eat. Doris," she said, turning to her daughter, "the roast is in the oven, the rest is already on the table. Anna, let's show the house to Johnny."

The thick red carpet from the stairs covered each sole of Johnny's feet as he went up step by step and grew taller and taller in the mirror that covered the whole wall at the top of the stairs. Upstairs, there were four doors on either side.

"Here, on the left. The second one is your bedroom," said Grandma Joan opening the door. "The next one is Anna's and the one on the end is her parents'. Mine is next to theirs," she said, pointing to the one at the end on the right. "And now, Anna, let's go to the basement to see if we can interest him in something," she said, joyfully winking in Johnny's direction.

"I'd rather rest on the bed for a while." Johnny looked around the room to evaluate it. "Is that the grandfather clock my father tried to open when he was five, to see who's moving the pendulum?" Johnny asked going toward the old clock.

"Oh, come on, child, you're young, you'll have plenty of time to rest afterwards! Yes, this is the clock Andrew, your father, told you about, and this was your father's room, but you'll have plenty of time to explore your father's past later. Now, come with me," Grandma Joan said grabbing Johnny's hand, "and let me show you something you've never seen before!"

On the main floor, hidden from sight by the main stairs, there was another set of stairs, going down to the basement. "We are going to the basement for a little while, Doris!" yelled Grandma Joan as they started descending.

"Don't be long, the roast is ready. I'm putting it on the table," Doris answered back.

"And now…" Grandma Joan turned to Johnny, "here it is: our Kimball Theatre Organ!" she said opening the door with a theatrical gesture.

As he stepped in, Johnny saw a very big instrument, taking up almost half the basement, with many big metal pipes and two levels of keys, forming a half circle, one above the other and one deeper than the other, looking like a strange two-in-one curved piano.

"Listen to this!" said Grandma Joan, sitting in front of the instrument.

"Come sit here on the sofa," Anna whispered to Johnny. "Grandma Joan loves the Kimball Theatre Organ. She could play it for hours!"

"Tu-tu-tu-tuuum!" a deep organ sound filled the air and Johnny recognized the beginning of Beethoven's Symphony No. 9. But not only the piano was heard, but also drums, violins, flutes and a lot of other instruments. Grandma Joan was just pressing the keys.

"This is called a horseshoe-shaped console, Johnny. It's a French design to allow the organist to reach any key or pedal while singing," explained Grandma Joan slowly moving to reach the keys. "It's a whole orchestra here: drums, chimes, violin, flute, oboe, marimbas, harp, xylophone and so on. Doesn't it sound great?"

Oh, wow, thought Johnny, *how did they fit this organ in here? It might have cost a fortune!* "It sounds great!" he answered.

"Mother, Johnny might be hungry and tired," said Doris entering the basement.

"Yes dear, of course. But first, let him hear this wonderful bird song," she said pressing a key, "isn't it wonderful?" Grandma Joan laughed while stepping out of the chair. "It always makes me laugh! Oh, Johnny," she said coming to him with her open arms, "you have no idea how glad I am that you came here. Christmas with all of you makes my old heart sing!" she said hugging and kissing Johnny's blond hair.

"Can I try to play it?" asked Johnny coming toward the Kimball Theatre Organ.

"Of course, Johnny, but not now... let's eat!" said Grandma Joan following Aunt Doris up the stairs.

Chapter 2

"Good morning, sleepy head!" said Anna standing up from an old black leather armchair. "I'm sorry, I couldn't wait any longer for you to wake up by yourself. Today we have to take the Christmas decorations out of the attic, and I can't wait! Mother put us in charge of this job until she gets back from work," she declared proudly, "and later on my father will come home from his derrick and we'll set the Christmas tree up and put on the lights... okay, Johnny, I'll let you get dressed. I'll be in the kitchen, breakfast is waiting. But please, hurry! By the way, there is a broken clock in the desk's right drawer – your father must have been very interested in how things work!" Anna said closing the door after her.

When the sound of Anna's steps was lost down the stairs, silence once again filled Johnny's room. Leaning on an elbow in his bed he looked through the window at the big snowflakes dancing on their way down.

Everything is so nice and with a special warmth here, but my heart feels like a stone, thought Johnny. *My father's room... He looks so young in those photographs on the wall! I guess he didn't know my mother back then! I wonder what my parents are doing now?* And the tears that filled his eyes helped lift a part of the heaviness from his soul. *Anna is nice and everybody seems happy that I came here. Maybe Aunt Doris is right that they needed this time alone to visit Europe. And here there is snow... I can make a snowman. I've never made one before. I wonder what building toys they have? Maybe I'll find some here, in my father's room. I have to check after breakfast. And the Christmas tree – I guess I won't be bored today.* Johnny continued his mind chatter while getting dressed. I hope Mum and Dad will call me today.

"Finally!" Anna stated when Johnny came to the kitchen. "Grandma Joan made a lot of food for us this morning but we still don't know what you like to eat."

"Usually milk and cereal, but today I would try to make something with this strip of bacon as a mouth and a boiled egg," he said cutting the egg in two halves and arranging it as two eyes. "I need a nose!" said Johnny reaching for a small carrot.

"What?" asked Anna coming to stand beside him at the table. "You're something else, you know that?" she said laughing. "And now you'll eat the smiley face you've made?"

"Of course!" Johnny tried to keep back his smile. "It's very tasty. You should try it for yourself!"

"Good morning, kids!" said Grandma Joan. "My heart is filled with joy looking at both of you!" she said patting their heads. "Now that you finished eating, go to the attic to choose the decorations for the Christmas tree, I have just set up the ladder for you. Be careful and don't lose too much time with the treasure!"

"What treasure?" asked Johnny curiously as they headed to the attic.

"The chest full of diamonds and gold and pearls from our great great great grandfather," Anna whispered grabbing Johnny's hand and looking seriously at him with her big eyes. And than she burst in laughing: "She meant all her past, I'll show you!"

The attic was unexpected for Johnny: old chairs, lamps, a mobile stand with dresses, a big piece of cardboard folded twice on the vertical, painted with trees, a lake and a house on it, books, a treadle sewing machine, a box with wigs, another one with wooden puppets, everything stuffed into each other.

Johnny grabbed one puppet and started to study the way it was made. Anna came by him: "Those puppets were made more then a hundred years ago! See now what Grandma Joan said about the treasure? We could stay here all day exploring! Grandma Joan's mother was an actress," Anna said, "and her brother was a painter. He made all the sets for his sister's movies, like the one on that wall," she said, pointing to the one with the trees and the lake. "At that time, the movies were made without sound, and the action was explained by the actor's movements, gesture, facial mimicry and the written passages."

"How do you know all of this?" asked Johnny.

"Because I ask and I listen. And this is my favorite part of the house – have you noticed the treadle sewing machine from that corner? Grandma Joan's mother made all of her dresses. I think they're so pretty!" Anna said moving a dress from the stand. "Oh, and over here are letters from her admirers – look at the beautiful handwriting!" she said taking an old and yellowed letter from its envelope.

"I'm more interested in how they made their toys back then. Look at this one!" Johnny said moving a stick at the back of another wooden puppet to make it move its hands and legs. "Do I hear the organ from the basement? What's it called?"

"Yes, it's the Kimball Theatre Organ; Grandma Joan plays it every day. The Kimball Theatre Organ was made around the same time as most of the stuff here. Grandma Joan bought it almost twenty years ago in her mother's memory, because all through her childhood Grandma Joan was among actors, their stories and their world. And because it's so big, they had to clear the basement to fit it in and this is how all of this old 'treasure' stuff got here, in the attic."

"Do you play it?" asked Johnny.

"The Theatre Organ? Not really, I only know what a few of the keys are for. But my brother, Michael knows — he will come tomorrow from the University for his Christmas break. He'll be happy to teach you – every year at Christmas he and Grandma Joan give us a concert.

Michael wants to be a piano teacher and he plays it really well! And he's so funny to be with, I really miss him when he's gone."

"The way I miss my parents now?" Johnny bent his head down. "My father also plays the piano, but not so much lately. He's tired all the time – maybe this is why they needed to be alone! Let's explore some more in here, I want to tell him everything when I go back home."

Anna smiled at Johnny. "Only for a little bit, we still have to choose the Christmas decorations and take them downstairs. As soon as my parents get home, we'll start with the lights and decorations. The house will look magical!"

Magical! thought Johnny. *Magic for me would be to find Mum and Dad downstairs!*

Chapter 3

"Good morning. Did my parents call yet?" asked Johnny as he sat down at the breakfast table the next day.

Anna was sitting by her father, Dennis Richardson, who was facing his wife, Aunt Doris and Grandma Joan was at the head of the table. Anna's parents exchanged a short look and then Aunt Doris answered: "Yes, they called while you were sleeping. They sent you their love, and they will call again when their schedule allows. Do you want a croissant, Johnny? Grandma Joan baked them this morning."

"I didn't hear the phone, when was it?" asked Grandma Joan.

"That's because I was by the phone when it started ringing and I answered immediately. Tea, anyone?"

"Can I call my parents now? I know their cell numbers!" Johnny pushed his chair to go to the phone.

"Johnny," Uncle Dennis stood in Johnny's way, "your parents said that they forgot to take the charger, so only they can call here."

"Why didn't you wake me up?" Johnny's eyes filled with tears.

"They may call later, Johnny. Don't be upset, eat now and I'll call you when they phone," Uncle Dennis turned back to his seat.

"Father, when will Michael be here?" Anna asked.

"He should be here any minute. And I'm sure he'll like the way we decorated the house and the Christmas tree. You've done a great job, kids!"

"Please tell him when he comes that we're in the library," said Anna putting her plate in the sink. "Breakfast was delicious, thank you!"

***

"This is, after the attic, my second favorite room." Anna opened the door and let Johnny go first.

"Oh, wow! All these books are real?" Johnny's eyes widened. "Three walls full of books? Who reads that much? There's even a rolling ladder to climb on to reach the books close to the ceiling!" He jumped on the ladder that started rolling towards the window.

"Johnny!" Anna screamed and rushed to stop it. "You have to be gentle, they are all old and you never know... The books might fall on you!"

"This is my favorite room in this house!" Johnny climbed down from the ladder. "I bet it was a scientist who built this room: the big desk in front of the window, and I bet this leather chair is comfortable!" he said sitting on it. "Two armchairs in front of the desk, most probably for discussing important business with clients. So many books clearly show how interested he was about learning more... Who built this library? Look!" Johnny said taking an old journal from one drawer of the desk. "What neat handwriting, what is that?"

"This was built by our grandfather, who was a doctor, and the journal you're holding in your hands is where he noted each consultation. Can you read it? Mother said that he had put his patients alphabetically for further reference, so he could have a history of the patient's illnesses." Anna sat in one of the armchairs in front of the desk with her legs crossed.

"This is so easily done now with a computer!" said Johnny flipping the pages.

"You know what, Johnny? Maybe you can be a doctor one day!" Anna said with her crystalline voice looking straight to Johnny as if picturing him being a doctor.

Jonathan let the journal stand in his lap, trying to fit in his imagination the picture of him as a doctor. "Yes, I could," he said hesitantly after a while. "But I like building so much, I guess I'll be a better builder than a doctor."

"Then maybe I should be a doctor, you'll be a builder and Michael a musician," Anna said.

The door opened and Johnny saw a thin young man, with shoulder length black curly hair and a big smile. "Michael, you're here!" Anna yelled jumping up and rushing into his arms. "This is our cousin Johnny, he likes to build."

"Really?" Michael's voice sounded comforting. "Nice to meet you, Johnny! I'm going to the stable, and then we can make a snowman. Are you coming?"

"Stable?" Johnny asked.

"They didn't show you the horses? Come with me, they are such wonderful creatures!" Michael put one hand over Anna's shoulders and the other over Johnny's. "But have you seen the Kimball Theatre Organ, Johnny?"

"Yes, Grandma Joan showed it to me the first day I came here. Can you teach me what all the keys do?" Johnny stopped in the main hall.

"Of course, how many years will you stay here?" Michel laughed, and in a small voice added, "I have a special song for tomorrow... did they tell you that on Christmas day, Grandma Joan and I are giving a concert, and each of us tries to find the best song for that?"

"Yes, can you play your song for me?" asked Johnny.

"Not yet, I don't want to spoil the surprise. Let's go now to the stable, and I'll tell you on the way about the Kimball Theatre Organ. What I found interesting," Michael started as they left the house, "is that one of the previous owners, Glenn White if I'm not mistaken, bought it for one thousand dollars from a flooded Theatre in Chehalis Washington, where the Theatre Organ was sitting in six inches of water! With his truck, it took him seven trips to transport all the numerous parts that make up the Kimball Theatre Organ. To fit the organ into his parents' basement, he had to chip a section out of the basement foundation to get the console in, and he also had to bend the pipes. All the restoration process took more than six years of his spare time. Can you imagine, six years of work till he could play it?"

"Did it take so long also to be installed in this basement? And who did it?" Johnny asked.

"No!" answered Michael, "I think Grandma Joan made an arrangement with the previous owner to have the Kimball Theatre Organ installed in her basement, and it didn't take more than a couple of weeks. Look, there is the stable, now let's see the horses. I'm sure you'll love them!"

It's good to have an older brother, especially a nice one like Michael! thought Johnny, looking at Anna. *I bet my father likes horses as well. After all, he grew up here! Oh, how much I want him to be here!*

CHAPTER 4

"The concert was amazing!" Johnny stayed to chat with Anna and Michael after the guests went back upstairs. "I can still feel the vibrations in my body, can't you?"

"Yes, I feel it every year after the Christmas concert," Michael said. "The Kimball Theatre Organ is such a powerful instrument, and this is a relatively small room. With so many people, it feels like we actually went to a real concert."

Johnny bent his head, looking at the floor. "My parents like music so much, I wish they were here. We always went together to concerts."

"Ah, here you are, kids!" said Uncle Dennis. "Whose song did you like better?" he winked in Michael's direction. "Come on, Johnny, you don't have to answer! Let's go up and Michael will tell you a little about our guests."

"Olivia!" Anna yelled happily when they reached the main floor. Running, the girl left them.

"Anna's friend, Olivia, has just come with her parents from their winter vacation. They came straight from the airport, but they couldn't be here in time for the concert," said Uncle Dennis before following Anna. "See you later, boys!"

Michael waved in Olivia's direction. "I guess the girls will chat all evening, so I won't be waiting for Anna to come back to start introducing our guests to you. There, in front of you, talking with Grandma Joan, is Mr. Sorensen and his wife, Barbara. He is the richest man in town and he always talks as though the world revolves around him. His mother, who died three years ago, was a close friend of Grandma Joan, so she always invites him out of respect for his mother. But let's talk about someone nice, like the Clarks, our closest neighbors." Michael pointed to the left corner. "They came here when I was five years old and their boy, Ben, was six. Ben and I played together. We learned to horseback ride together; we even learned to play the Kimball Theatre Organ together. But he wanted to be a doctor and was accepted at Harvard Medical School. Now he's studying for his final exams and is also working in an Emergency Room. That's why he didn't come home this Christmas."

"Nice that your friend lived so close to you." Johnny put his hands into his pockets. "I don't see my best friend Aidan much. We go to the same school and play and talk together every recess. His mother is the physical education teacher in our school."

"Hello, Michael," a woman in an old fashioned dress said, as she walked toward them, with a big smile. "It's so nice to see you! Your technique has improved so much from last year. You must have very good teachers at the University." The woman warmly hugged Michael and then turned to Johnny. "And you, young man, are you Andrew Pearl's son?" As Johnny nodded, she continued, "You resemble him so much when he was your age! Is he still practicing piano daily? Where is he, I haven't seen him tonight," she said looking one more time throughout the room.

For a moment, Johnny wanted to answer: *And who are you to ask me anything?* But her face and her kindness stopped him from being rude. *I don't even know where they are, exactly,* he thought.

"They... my parents are in Europe!" he answered instead, squeezing his fists, while struggling to keep his tears in check.

"And this sweet lady," Michael smiled, turning toward her, "is Miss Beatrice, our dear piano teacher. Johnny, your father was her first student and she always talked about him as an example."

"Well, because he studied hard and he had so many questions... It was a pleasure to teach him, I wish all my students were so curious and willing to learn!"

"I see you've met Johnny, Beatrice," Grandma Joan said, joining the little group. "I am glad to be with you. I can't believe how rude this Sorensen became – he asked me again to sell him the Kimball Theatre Organ! Well, you know, Beatrice how nice Grace, his mother, was and I am glad that we were friends, but this boy is... I don't even want to think about him anymore! I guess I have to cease inviting him to our Christmas concerts; we will be better without him!"

"We're going to get something to eat now, Grandma Joan," said Michael grabbing Johnny's shoulders. "Are you coming with us, Miss Beatrice? The cheese platters looked amazing and the sausage rolls smelled delicious when Mother took them out of the oven – I can't wait to taste them!"

"You, boys, always ready to hunt something, at least for your stomach! Thank you, but I will stay a little longer to chat here. I hope I will see you again in the next days." Miss Beatrice smiled and she put her hand over her heart. "You made me proud of you tonight, Michael!"

"What an open hearted teacher!" exclaimed Johnny on their way to the food table.

"This is the benefit of living in a small town: we know and care for each other, well, with small exceptions, of course!" Michael implied looking at Mr. Sorensen as they got close to him. "All this nice atmosphere here and he is always thinking about his business and trying to take advantage of someone. Good that he had his back to us, so we don't have to greet him!" Michael whispered in Johnny's ear.

But just then Mr. Sorensen grabbed the arm of the man he was talking to, and pushed him away. "You have to. Listen to me – do it tonight!" and his whisper felt to Johnny like a chill in the air. Mr. Sorensen turned around, but stopped, bewildered as he saw Michael. His face was turning red.

I guess he didn't mean for anybody else to hear this, thought Johnny. *What is going on here?*

"What? Are you spying on me? I always have to force this good for nothing driver of mine to do his job! If I ask him to... wash my car tonight, he'll have to do it!" Mr. Sorensen said in a withering tone. "I had enough here! Adam," he yelled turning to his driver, "take me home now and you'll take care of the car later! Inform my wife that we're leaving and let's go."

"You were so right about him!" Johnny said to Michael, while looking as Mr. Sorensen spun on his heel and walked away. "To ask his driver to wash his car after the Christmas concert, when everybody is celebrating..." Johnny stopped for a moment as a thought popped up in his mind. "I acted not very much differently when I first got here," he said, "because I was upset that my parents didn't take me with them on their trip to Europe. But all of you welcomed me in such a wonderful way. I haven't really had time to think very much about them. Maybe Mr. Sorensen acts that way because something is missing in his life."

"Yes, his manners!" laughed Michael.

Chapter 5

"Fire! Wake up, Michael, the stable is burning!" Johnny cried.

"What? Johnny, is it you?" Michael tried to keep his eyes open. "The stable?" He took off his blanket, jumped out of the bed and pulled on his clothes. "Johnny, go wake up the rest of the house and tell my father I'm outside connecting the water hose. Tell him to phone the fire department," he said rushing out the door with Johnny at his heels.

Johnny rushed to his aunt and uncle's bedroom, knocked on the door loudly, opened it and shouted: "Wake up, Uncle Dennis, the stable is on fire! Michael is setting up the water hose. I'll wake up Anna."

"What?" Aunt Doris jumped out of bed and put on her dressing gown. "Oh, Johnny, I'll go wake up my mother. Did Michael phone for help?"

"No, Aunt Doris, he said we have to," Johnny said going to Anna's door, but Anna was already standing in the hall. "What's all this noise?" she asked.

"The stable, the stable are burning! Get dressed quickly, and let's go see how we can help," Johnny said, rushing back to his room to dress.

"Meet me downstairs," said Uncle Dennis.

"Mother, keep Anna with you and call the fire department. Johnny and Doris, let's go outside to help Michael," he said and opened the door.

"I think the water froze in the pipes, the valve was so hard to move... I hope I didn't open it enough, otherwise... " Michael moved to let his father try.

"No, Michael, you opened the valve, but the water is frozen here!" Uncle Dennis stood up, looked for a few seconds to the stable, and then turned back. "Doris, take Johnny and go to the Clark's for help. Michael, come with me to take out the horses."

"Boys... be careful!" said Aunt Doris, taking Johnny's hand and going to the car. "It's not too far to the Clark's," she said, speeding her steps even more, "but it's faster with the car. And from there we might go to the Johnston's as well. But how did we find out about the fire?" She turned toward Johnny while opening the car door.

"Actually, I couldn't sleep," Johnny said as he fastened his seat belt. "I was thinking about my parents and the Christmas concert and all of a sudden my room got lighter and lighter. When I went by the window, I saw the red-yellow tongues of fire coming from the direction of the stable and I heard the horses whinnying, and then I woke up Michael and you."

"So if the house did not burn down as well we owe it to you!" said Aunt Doris after a few moments of driving in silence. "Here is the Clark's house. Stay here, I'll be back quickly."

If I was with my parents in Europe now, they might not have known in time about the fire. Aunt Doris might be right, the fire could also spread to the house, and if they were sleeping... Even if I miss my parents, now I am glad they didn't take me with them. I hope Uncle Dennis and Michael will get the horses out in time. The firemen will be there shortly, I can hear their sirens in the distance, coming closer. I wish I could help more, he thought as his aunt slid back into the driver's seat.

"The Clarks will come to the stable to help with the horses. They called the Johnston's and they're coming as well, so we will go back home now," Aunt Doris said and started the car.

"The light from the fire is even brighter! I hope they are okay," Johnny cried. They could see the flames from the road. As soon as they pulled into the driveway, Aunt Doris jumped out and ran toward the stable. Johnny followed her closely.

"You saved Spark!" Aunt Doris took the horse's reins from Michael's hand, and tried to calm the frightened horse. "Mr. Clark and Mr. Johnston will be here shortly. Oh! Here they are!"

"Mother, take Spark around the house where he won't see the flames. Come!" Michael turned back to the burning stable followed by Mr. Clark and Mr. Johnston.

"Anita and Sandra, wait here for the next horses," Aunt Doris said to Mrs. Clark and Mrs. Johnston. "Johnny, come with me." Aunt Doris firmly pulled the reins as Spark was still kicking and jumping. "Come on, Spark, you're saved!"

"The sirens from the fire truck sound so close! Is that their flashing lights? Look, Aunt Doris, the firemen have arrived!" Johnny pointed happily to the truck.

"It seems they have time to save all the horses," Mrs. Clark said coming with Mrs. Johnston with another two horses. "The other four horses the boys are coming with, two of them were just pulled out from the stable as we left to come here. Poor frantic animals, they were lucky you were able to mobilize in time!"

"Johnny was the one who alerted us all, my hero!" Aunt Doris looked gratefully to Johnny.

"Everybody out of the way!" the firemen pulled the fire hose.

"Can I go look at them?" Johnny asked Aunt Doris.

"Yes, Johnny, but keep your distance."

"Have you rescued all the horses?" the fire chief asked Uncle Dennis.

"Yes, this is the last one, but they inhaled a lot of smoke!"

"When you opened the stable's doors, you added more oxygen and fed the flames. Now let's put this fire down!" the chief ordered his team.

"Come with me now, Johnny," Uncle Dennis stopped to remove the black smoke from his face with his handkerchief. "We've done as much as we could here. Now we have to figure out where we can keep the horses."

What wonderful creatures are these horses, strong and beautiful, yet they need so much love and care! It's amazing how they gathered so many people to their rescue! Uncle Dennis looks so tired and he is coughing from the smoke, but he and all the others will still endure the cold to take care of the horses, thought Johnny.

"Dennis," said Aunt Doris when they joined the group, "Mr. Johnston said he can keep the horses for tonight in his old barn and Michael will stay there to calm them. We need blankets, because the walls are made out of wood. And tomorrow we have to ask Mr. Sorensen if he can keep our horses for a while, as we don't know anyone else who has a stable."

Chapter 6

"Johnny, please ask everybody to come into the dinning room. We have matters to discuss," Grandma Joan said as she took off her coat. Her lips were tight and her eyebrows were pulled together in a frown.

"As you know, Dennis and I went to see Mr. Sorensen," she stated firmly when Aunt Doris, Johnny and Anna had taken their places at the dinning table. "He wasn't supportive at all of our circumstances. In fact, he used it to try one more time to persuade me to sell him the Kimball Theatre Organ." Grandma Joan paused to look at each member of the family.

"I wanted you all to be here," she continued with a determined look, "because I want to listen to everybody's opinion whether we should sell him the organ or not. As you know, he is the only one who has a stable where we could keep our horses, but he won't accept them unless I agree to sell the Kimball Theatre Organ."

"What a cruel person!" Johnny said.

"Michael, we're in the dining room!" Aunt Doris called when she heard the front door. "How are the horses?" she asked as soon as he entered the room.

"They are in obvious stress, and it's very cold in the barn. The blankets helped, but it's not enough. Mr. Sorensen agreed to keep them in his stable?"

"Only if Grandma Joan will sell the Kimball Theatre Organ to him!" Uncle Dennis showed Michael a chair. "Sit for a little while. We all have to decide together what we can do with the horses. Johnston's barn is too cold for them, Mr. Sorensen is not a solution, so should we consider selling the horses?"

"Please, Father, don't sell them, I love them!" Anna put her hands together in a prayerful way as her eyes filled with tears.

"Doris, I think we have to phone your brother," Grandma Joan said.

"No!" Aunt Doris jumped out of her chair.

"What's wrong with you, dear?" Grandma Joan asked, surprised. "Don't you think Johnny's father has a say in this? After all, the horses are his, too, even if he didn't have time to come here at all in the last four years."

"Sorry, I guess I'm stressed as well as tired. Of course I think he also has the right to his opinion about that, but not today," she said looking at her husband. "We don't have to spoil his vacation with such bad news. Besides, I think now they might be at a concert."

"In France they are nine hours ahead of us, so it's evening already there," added Uncle Dennis.

"They didn't call me today," Johnny said, surprised. "I wonder why?"

"Maybe they called while we were sleeping and we didn't hear the phone ringing as we were all so tired," Uncle Dennis said and then continued, "Anyway, I don't think Johnny's parents will disagree with any decision we make."

"I remember when I came here from the airport I saw some horses in the field." Johnny looked at his uncle. "Are those horses sleeping in that field?"

Uncle Dennis looked at Johnny in surprise. "Sometimes you have to have a child's mind to see what's right in front of you!" he said and Johnny felt like the stale air in the room started to move again. "Of course horses will survive the cold, as long as they have enough food! My father told me that when I was your age, Johnny. The horse's body heats itself as it metabolizes the food; without food, the horse will freeze to death," he said, sounding excited. "Mother, we don't have to sell the Kimball Theatre Organ at all, we will just ask the Johnston's to keep the horses for a while, until we can rebuild our stable!"

"But I slept there last night, and it's very cold and the horses really were stressed!" Michael said. "Besides, we can't rebuild the stable soon, as the ground is frozen!"

"Michael, the horses were wild animals once. They had to adapt to cold, and this is why they grew a thick coat for the winter. We keep them in the stable all the time, so I forgot they can survive the cold. The stress was from the fire, because they were so scared, but this will pass in the next few days, with our love and care," Uncle Dennis said and smiled. "And when the weather will allow us, we'll start working at the new stable."

"We have to ride them every day, or at least take them for a walk, right?" Anna asked.

"Of course, dear," Aunt Doris answered. "This we won't change. And, as your father said, we will still love them and care for them. What I don't understand is how the fire started?"

"My dear family," said Grandma Joan, "we are all tired. The fire-fighters will tell us in the next few days what happened. Why waste our day making suppositions? Dennis, please call Mr. Johnston to ask if he will agree to keep the horses until we rebuild our stable. Doris and I will prepare something to eat, and I want everybody to get dressed properly, as we will celebrate the second day of Christmas. Time will tell what else is to be done, but for now, let's be happy that we are all well and together. That's the most important thing. And Michael, maybe after lunch, we will play the Kimball Theatre Organ again," she said winking at Michael.

Chapter 7

"One more lap, Michael, please!" Anna pleaded from Spark's saddle. "And then Spark is all yours, Johnny, I promise!"

Michael kept Spark's reins, "You know we have to walk all the horses, Anna, not only Spark, even if it's your favorite. Now is not the time for us to play, but to comfort them as much as we can," he said helping Anna get off the horse's back.

"But if we have three reins, we can walk three horses at once. I don't have to ride them," said Johnny. "I mean, I can wait till tomorrow to ride a horse."

"Johnny, I cannot let you or Anna take the reins. You are both still too young for this," Michael said smiling. "But I like the way you always try to find a solution for everything you encounter."

"Father!" Anna yelled and ran into Mr. Richardson's arms.

"Hello, kids, it's time for you to go back home now," Uncle Dennis said with a smile as he pulled Anna's hat over her eyes. "Doris is waiting for you to help her set the table. Michael and I will be coming after we finish walking all the horses."

"See you soon!" Anna turned around and started running.

"One moment!" Uncle Dennis came in Johnny's direction. "Your parents called a half an hour ago, Johnny. They are waiting for you to call them back. Say hello from us."

"I will, Uncle Dennis. See you later." Johnny left happily to catch up with Anna.

"You still miss them, don't you?" Anna looked serious at Johnny. "Even if you didn't have so much time to think about them lately, I know you miss them."

"A lot!" Johnny sighed and looked down. "But now I'm glad I've had the chance to get to know all of you."

"Usually we don't get so much agitation after the Christmas party, but this year because of the fire, everything is different. You didn't even have a chance to talk to your parents yet. Did they know about the fire? My father must have been... What's shining over there?" Anna pointed on the left of the path.

"Let's see. Maybe a coin?" supposed Johnny.

"A coin? On the snow? And who could have lost it? It's a little far from the path we take to and from the Johnston's. A button!" Anna leaned down to take it.

"Look, Anna, footprints! Let's follow them to see where they go," Johnny said. "I'm feeling like an explorer!" he said bursting into laughter.

"Well, of course!" said Anna when she could see the place where the stable had stood a few days before. "Maybe Michael lost it. I'll ask him when he comes back home." Anna put the button into her pocket.

"Let's go, Anna. I can't wait to talk to my parents!" Johnny said grabbing Anna's hand. "I bet my mother is concerned because of the fire. She is so protective!" Johnny opened the front door and let Anna enter first.

"Mother, we're back!" Anna said loudly.

"Hmm!" Johnny filled his lungs with the delicious smell. "They've baked bread!"

"It's true, Johnny," Aunt Doris came from the kitchen door wiping her hands. "And this for me is the best smell ever! Lunch is almost ready. Wash your hands and come into the kitchen," she said going back.

"My mother makes bread too," Johnny said taking off his jacket and snow pants. "Not so often though. She is busy with her work."

"Why is my father ringing the bell?" said Anna turning back from the stairs. "I'll get it, Mom!"

"Where is your Grandma Joan?" Mr. Sorensen said with an echoing cry when Anna opened the door. "Don't just stay there, let us in and go get her!" he said closing the door and looking all around.

"What's the matter?" Grandma Joan came from the kitchen, followed by Aunt Doris. "Oh, good afternoon, Mr. Sorensen, what makes you come by?" Grandma Joan looked curiously at Mr. Sorensen and the other man. "And who did you bring with you?"

"I came with the appraiser, Mr. Chan. And it's not an easy job to find one, especially this time of the year!" Mr. Sorensen said proudly.

"I don't understand. Why are you here with an appraiser?" Grandma Joan looked at Aunt Doris and then back to Mr. Sorensen. "How can we help you?"

"Don't pretend you don't understand. I told you I will take your horses into my stable only if you will sell me the Kimball Theatre Organ. I came with the appraiser to know what it's worth. Show us the way."

Grandma Joan's face turned white, and then red. She straightened her spine and spoke with an icy tone, "How dare you to come into my house and give me orders? I never said I will sell you the Kimball Theatre Organ, and I never will. Now get out!"

"I'm sorry, Mr. Appraiser," she said turning to Mr. Chan. "I'm sure you don't deserve to be in a situation like this, and frankly, neither do we. Goodbye," she said opening the door for them.

"You'll be sorry for this!" Mr. Sorensen turned and left, followed by Mr. Chan.

"No, I won't," said Grandma Joan closing the door. She looked a few moments at Doris, Johnny and Anna, then took one of Anna and Johnny's hands into hers, looked in their eyes and said: "Kids, what I want you to understand from this awkward situation is that nobody can tell you what to do or how you should feel. I won't be sorry, because I won't spend my time and energy being sorry. I made my decision in keeping the Kimball Theatre Organ, and I am quite happy with it. The only thing I am sorry for is that this Sorensen kidnapped a part of the joy of this day, but it's up to us to restore it. Let's go set up the table and be happy for being together," she said. Smiling, she took Johnny and Anna with her to the kitchen.

CHAPTER 8

"Johnny, have you called your parents?" asked Uncle Dennis as he came with Michael into the dinning room.

"No, Dennis, we had no time." Aunt Doris put the pot with the soup in the centre of the table. "He'll call them after lunch. Let's eat now while the food is hot."

The ringing of the phone made Johnny jump from his chair.

"I'll get the phone," said Grandma Joan who was closer to it. "Michael, it's for you," she said giving the phone's handset to Michael. "I thought..."

"That it would be my parents," Johnny said, finishing her sentence. "Yes, me too."

"This soup is so good, Grandma Joan," Anna grabbed another slice of bread.

"Do you remember I told you that I invited my teacher, Mr. Williams," said Michael looking at his parents while taking his place back at the table, "and he said he had some other previous plans for the holiday? Well, something was cancelled and he will come here tomorrow. He knows so much about the history of music; you'll like how passionate he is about explaining it! And he is curious to see the

Kimball Theatre Organ I told him so much about. Grandma Joan, can we play again the pieces we prepared for the Christmas Concert while he's here?"

"Of course, darling, I understand you are excited, but eat now." Grandma Joan stood up to remove the soup plates, followed by Aunt Doris.

"Oh, and Michael," Johnny remembered, "on the way back Anna found a button; it might be yours. It was a little further apart from the path. We saw it because it was shining on the snow."

"I don't remember a missing button on my coat. I'll check after I finish this delicious steak," he said.

"No, it's not mine," Michael said, when he returned after checking his coat. "Now are we going to practice more on the Kimball Theatre Organ for tomorrow, Grandma?"

"Michael, we had a situation here with Mr. Sorensen, and Johnny didn't get to talk with his parents yet," said Aunt Doris looking at her husband. "Please, everybody, be seated for a while, I have something to tell you."

"Now, what else can it be, dear?" Grandma Joan dropped into her chair.

"Johnny," Aunt Doris started, "you are a big boy now, so I hope you will understand. Your father had surgery this morning, and the doctors said it was successful."

"What?" Johnny and Grandma Joan yelled at the same time. Johnny's tears started to fall on his cheek while he tightened his hands on the table.

His father's migraines and the days he was too tired to go to work – Johnny recalled his memories – *and the day they had to see the doctor... Oh, no, he really was sick!* Johnny pressed his hands against his head to stop remembering.

"What... what was wrong with him?" Johnny could hardly articulate.

"He had a brain tumor. Luckily his doctor was able to schedule the surgery soon after he discovered it. And Mother," Aunt Doris said, turning to Grandma Joan, "we all agreed we didn't want you to worry.

The way we know you, you would have taken the first plane to be with him, and Johnny wouldn't have had the experience of a Christmas here."

"And what a Christmas it was!" added Uncle Dennis.

"That's why you didn't want to call your brother, Doris, when we discussed whether to keep the horses or to sell them!" Grandma Joan realized. "Don't hide anything from me, Doris. You know I like to ask for your opinions before deciding anything."

"You're right, mother," Aunt Doris took Grandma Joan's hands into hers, "but this was an unusual situation and I wanted to spare you from the anxiety and uncertainty."

"Johnny," Aunt Doris said. She moved around the table to comfort him. "Your mother couldn't call you as she was afraid you would pick up from her voice that something was wrong. Maybe it's better to let your mother rest for now, and wait until she calls us again, even if it's tomorrow."

"Are you OK, Johnny?" Anna took one of his hands into hers.

"I... I don't know! I knew he had headaches, and he was tired all the time, and we had not played or talked so much lately, but, but..." his eyes filled with tears again. "I miss him very much and I want to tell him how much I love him!"

"I know he can feel your love, and that is all he needs right now. All our love and support." Uncle Dennis came to hug Johnny. "Johnny, your mother and father thought it would be best for you to think they were in Europe, even if you were upset they left without you. They knew you'd like it here, and I hope we made you feel at home, even if we had our unexpected challenges."

Chapter 9

"I can't believe tomorrow is New Year's Eve!" Johnny stopped walking and turned to Anna. "And after three more days I will go back home – I'm so grateful that my father is better and better every day!" He smiled and threw himself on the snow, and started making a snow angel.

"So, you're eager to go!" Anna teased. "Let's go back home now," she said shaking the snow off the back of Johnny's coat.

"I really like being here with you, and I really like snow, so I guess I'll ask my parents to let me come here again next year. Hopefully, there will not be ups and downs next time!" Johnny laughed and started running.

"Your cheeks are all red," Johnny said looking at Anna. "Let's walk now; we're almost home."

"I like running." Anna drew in her breath. "Look, Johnny, a car is coming to our house!" she said speeding up. "I wonder who can it be?"

"It's a firefighter!" Johnny recognized the uniform of the man who got out of the car. "I hope everything is okay. The firefighter came with his own car," he continued.

"Don't run. I'm waiting for you, kids." Grandma Joan stepped back to let the firefighter enter the house. "What red cheeks you kids have!" she said when Johnny and Anna arrived at the door.

A sound of grinding wheels made them look down the stairs. Another car stopped and Adam, Mr. Sorensen's driver got out of the car, sidestepped it and opened the door for Mr. Sorensen.

"The button, the button Johnny!" Anna nervously whispered to Johnny, shaking his hand. "Look, they are shining like the one we found. And there is one missing!" she said with a frightened look to Johnny.

"Let's go inside, Anna." Johnny pulled Anna in the house and at the back of the door.

"I will make one more try to persuade you to sell me the Kimball Theatre Organ," Mr. Sorensen said to Grandma Joan when he finished climbing the stairs. "I see you have guests," he said looking at the firefighter. "Where we can be undisturbed to discuss business?" Mr. Sorensen looked around.

"Nowhere, Mr. Sorensen." Grandma Joan gave him a cold look. "We have nothing to discuss as I have no intention of selling anything to you. You are not welcome here anymore. Don't ever come here again," she said closing the door in his face.

"Excuse me for letting you wait so long," Grandma Joan turned to the firefighter when she saw Anna and Johnny's scared faces. "What's the matter with you, kids? Anna, why are you trembling?" she said coming towards the kids to hug them.

"We... We..." Anna tried to explain.

"We saw that Mr. Sorensen's driver had a missing button on his coat, and the rest of the buttons were the same as the one we found a few days ago on the snow, not far from the burnt stable," Johnny explained.

"And where is that button?" The firefighter sounded interested. "I came to tell you," he said, looking at Grandma Joan, "that we finished our investigation and our conclusion is that it wasn't an accident. If you will give me the button you found, I'll be glad to give it to the police chief, to attach to the report I've just submitted before coming here, the one regarding your stable."

"So it's possible that he set the fire at the stable to make me sell him the Kimball Theatre Organ? What kind of person could do such a thing?" Grandma Joan looked at the firefighter.

"A dangerous one, madam!" The firefighter looked at the kids. "I hope Mr. Sorensen and his driver don't suspect you found a piece of evidence."

"I don't think so." Johnny tried to remember. "The driver was not looking at us, and neither was Mr. Sorensen."

"I need a small bag to put the button in. Just show me where it is and I will put it inside the bag to preserve the fingerprints on it; who knows, the lab may still find at least a partial fingerprint of the driver. And you know what," the firefighter said turning to Grandma Joan, "why don't you all come with me to the police station? They will need to know where and when the kids found the button."

"Yes, of course," said Grandma Joan. "Let me get my coat, and we will come with you. Let's finish this once and for all."

CHAPTER 10

"And then, after the chief police officer listened to the kids," Grandma Joan said as she finished relating to Uncle Dennis, Aunt Doris, Michael and Mr. Williams, Michael's teacher, what happened, "he came back with a few of his crew to see where the kids found the button. We left them working and returned home. Probably they will send for Mr. Sorensen and his driver today to start questioning them."

"This pushy Mr. Sorensen, maybe if he hadn't come today to try convincing you one more time to sell him the Kimball Theatre Organ, nobody would have known what he did to have it," Uncle Dennis was thinking out loud.

"Is he such a good musician that he wanted the Kimball Theatre Organ so much?" Mr. Williams wondered aloud.

"A good musician?" Uncle Dennis burst in laughter. "He has no idea what music is. He just thinks that if he wants something he can have it. He would probably pay somebody to play it."

"I think that Kimball Theatre Organ is a very good instrument, very well attuned," Mr. Williams said pouring more tea in his cup. "My suggestion is, whenever you no longer want it, please also consider donating it. Our University donated an old piano only a few months ago to the National Music Centre, located in Calgary, not too far from here. I was designated to go with the delivery truck to make sure the piano arrived in good condition. I saw all the exhibits in the National Music Centre and I can tell you it was impressive. I don't want to influence you, after all you've been through because of Mr. Sorensen and his greed for the Kimball Theatre Organ. You really deserve to enjoy its music, as it really seems to be part of your family."

"Cookies, anybody? More tea?" Aunt Doris lifted the cookie plate. "By the way, Johnny, while you were at the police station your mother called with good news. The doctors decided to release your father, so you will find him home when you go back. Isn't it wonderful?"

"Today is the best day ever!" Johnny ran to hug Aunt Doris. "I can't wait to see my parents and to tell them how wonderful it was for me to be here with all of you!"

"And maybe you'll come here again?" Aunt Doris smiled at him.

"For sure! If my parents can't come, I'll ask them to let me come. Now I know the way." Johnny went on hugging everybody.

"I didn't understand when I first came here what a wonderful family I have," Johnny said looking at each of them, "but now I do. Thank you!"

"Oh, Johnny, all these days with you were special for us too," Grandma Joan said fluffing Johnny's hair.

"And you're right, Mr. Williams," Grandma Joan said. "It may be the time to let other people enjoy the Kimball Theatre Organ. We had it for nineteen years already, and I am not growing younger. Michael, most probably will not come here to teach after he graduates, so the Kimball Theatre Organ will be forgotten. In my opinion, to let people admire it is more important than selling it. What do you think?"

"I think that is the right decision," Uncle Dennis nodded vigorously to strengthen the words. "But Michael has the right to his own decision. Anyway, I would say, let's keep it for one more year, and after the Christmas Concert we will ask you, Mr. Williams, to help us with the papers and transportation. What do you think, Michael?"

"I'm for it, of course! National Music Centre – what better place for the Kimball Theatre Organ can there be?" Michael answered excitedly.

"Then it's settled. The Kimball Theatre Organ will go to the National Music Centre," Grandma Joan concluded.

"And I'll be more than happy to help you in the process of donating the Kimball Theatre Organ." Mr. Williams smiled and shook Grandma Joan's hand.

AFTERWORD

Imagine a place of stillness, a place where you can see and feel the past, a place with so many stories waiting to be unraveled. Come with me, look, here is a violin, and another one over there. And there, some pianos, and keyboards, and a hummer-dulcimer. This is a Theremin, and there, look, it's the Kimball Theatre Organ! Sst! Be silent, the music of the past sleeps in these instruments!

Even though what you've just read was just a fiction story, the Kimball Theatre Organ is indeed one of the many musical instruments found within the collections at the National Music Centre in Calgary, AB.

Its history starts in 1924, when the organ was installed in St. Helen's Theater, Chehalis, Washington. The first private owner, Mr. Glen D. White Jr. acquired the Kimball Theatre Organ in 1952 for the sum of USD$1,000.00 from the flooded Chehalis Theatre in Washington, where the organ was sitting in six inches of water. It took seven trips for a truck to transport the numerous parts that make up the organ. Mr. White had to chip a section out of the basement's concrete wall in order to get the console into his parents' basement and to bend the pipes so the organ could be set up in the eight-foot height room. The restoration took him more than six years.

In 1962 the Kimball Theatre Organ was sold to Reginald Stone, (a popular British theatre organist) who commissioned White to install it in the Fox Theatre, Victoria, BC, Canada, where it accompanied silent films and presented concerts.

In 1966 the Kimball Theatre Organ was acquired and moved to Burnaby, BC, Canada.

In 1981 the Kimball Theatre Organ was acquired and moved to St. Albert, AB, Canada. It was later donated to the National Music Centre by Carol and Dave Otto in April 1999.

The roots of National Music Centre and its collection can be traced to the installation of a pipe organ (known as the Carthy Organ) in Calgary's Jack Singer Concert Hall in 1987. This instrument was built in Saint – Hyacinthe, Quebec, by Casavant Frères Ltd, which is Canada's oldest continuously operating musical instrument company. This installation of this instrument was the genesis of the International Organ Festival and Competition operated by TriumphEnt from 1990 to 2002. It also subsequently inspired the creation of a new organization known as the Chinook Keyboard Centre, which began developing a collection of keyboard instruments in mid-1996.

Chinook Keyboard Centre was soon renamed Cantos Music Museum and expanded the scope of its collection beyond keyboard instruments to include electronic instruments and sound equipment beginning in the year 2000, it also began to offer limited programming in the way of gallery tours and concerts.

In 2003, TriumphEnt and Cantos Music Museum joined forces to become the Cantos Music Foundation, and expanded its presentation of music programs using the collection and gallery spaces. In 2005, an exhibition commemorating 100 years of music in Alberta to mark the Centennial planted the seed to expand the organization's scope to chronicle, celebrate and foster a broader vision for music in Canada. And so, in February 2012, Cantos became the National Music Centre.

[http://www.nmc.ca/about/our-history]

Come, from near and far, feel the stillness, the stories and the music from the National Music Centre's instruments. And then, keep the music alive with you, everywhere you go!

Printed in Canada